IT MUST BE FATE

Also by Alexandria Blaelock

SHORT STORY COLLECTIONS
The Histories of Hayward Hall
Lovelorn, Lovestruck and Love at First Sight
Common or Garden Variety Heroes
Case Files of the Wilkinson Detective Agency
Unavoidable Fates
Christmas Travesties
Five Faces of Felicia Clarke
Little Place Called Home
Security Directorate Dossiers v. 1.
Security Directorate Dossiers v. 2.

FICTION
That Love Nonsense
Taipan vs Brown
The Ghost and Ms Cox
Friends Like That
Weaving the Wildwood
Wolf vs Orb

MS BLAELOCK'S BOOKS
Stress Free Dinner Parties
Signature Wardrobe Planning
Holistic Personal Finance
Minimally Viable Housekeeping
Planning a Life Worth Living

PICTURE BOOKS
Australia Felix

SELECTED SHORT STORIES
Alma's Grace
Blood and Bloody Profanity
Cancelled by the Cartel
Dingo Hunting
Honoris Virilis Respectu
Mince Pie Mystery
Remains of Christmas

IT MUST BE FATE

A FATES SHORT STORY

ALEXANDRIA BLAELOCK

BlueMere Books
MELBOURNE, AUSTRALIA

For permission requests, please contact enquiries@bluemerebooks.com.

Ordering Information:
Discounts are available on quantity purchases. For details, contact orders@bluemerebooks.com.

It Must Be Fate/Alexandria Blaelock
paperback ISBN: 978-1-923083-14-1
digital ISBN: 978-1-923083-15-8

Book Layout © BookDesignTemplates.com
Cover Art © Warm_Tail licenced from Shutterstock.com

IT MUST BE FATE

Laura bustled down the city street, sleek black handbag over one shoulder, stilettos clacking on the pavement.

Her shoulder-length black hair was smoothed back into an unravelling ponytail which swung from side to side with each step she took.

She looked the peak of efficiency in her slightly too tight black suit; anyone who looked at her would have thought she was at the pinnacle of her Personal Assistant career.

Perhaps her boss was the CEO of a medium-sized company who'd taken her with him to the top.

But she was uncomfortably aware she was perspiring, her feet were killing her, and she just wanted the time to sit somewhere, slip her shoes off and enjoy a *very* large, *very* cold and preferably alcoholic drink.

She balanced a packet of tomato sauce flavoured chips on top of her mobile phone in her left hand, crushing handfuls into her mouth with her right as she walked.

Not for the first time, she thought losing weight might be a good thing, but she just didn't have the time.

Not like the old days when she'd enjoyed cooking from scratch and taking long treks through the countryside hunting game.

And her sisters were useless - no help whatsoever.

Maybe next time they should go to Tokyo or Seoul where you could get healthier meals and snacks in every corner store.

Much more convenient, and so easy to keep the weight off.

Glass skyscrapers towered above her on all sides, reflecting the summer light and heat towards each other, and anyone unfortunate to be walking or waiting beneath them.

The air, barely cooled by the wind tunnelling along the street brought grit, sheets of newspaper, and empty chip packets with it.

She dropped her own empty packet into a bin, and the wind lifted it out again, threw it at her and then further on down the street where it joined a maelstrom of others.

Still walking, she lifted a handkerchief from her bag, wiped her hands on it and carefully put it back in case the wind took it as well.

She paused at a traffic light to check her phone.

In many ways, it was so handy to receive people's wishes by text, or perhaps a phone call now and again, but it was *too* easy for them.

She'd had to turn off the ring *and* the vibration, because it was a constant torment of noise.

In the old days, they'd wait for people to come to them, and because the journey was arduous, they didn't unless they had meaningful concerns.

She'd had the time to eat and exercise, and keep the house immaculately clean.

But now...

There was nowhere to hide out of reach, people used their wishes recklessly, and she couldn't keep up with them.

Let alone keeping the house in order and taking care of herself.

Not for the first time, she contemplated how much happier she might have been in an ordinary finite life.

A life full of all the frivolous concerns people had these days.

She started flicking through the texts:

Yes, doing well at the job interview.

No, definitely pregnant.

Yes, passing exams.

No, he doesn't like you; he's just scamming you.

Yes, she does like you; obsessively so.

She heard the lights change to walk, took a step forward and still focused on her phone, tripped over the curb.

Arms wheeling, she tried to save herself, but it looked like the ground was coming closer towards her anyway.

At the last possible minute, someone who smelled fresh and citrusy grabbed her arm, pulling her up, twisting her around and setting her on her feet.

A man.

A gorgeous man.

In an immaculately tailored navy-blue pinstripe suit. With a white shirt and matching vest if you please. A slim silver and blue diagonal stripe tie completed the picture.

His short, dark hair was neat and completely unaffected by the wind. It didn't look weighed down with product, nor did it look as though he'd spent any time in the bathroom blow-drying it.

Clean-shaven, with intriguingly green eyes.

Laura realised she was staring open-mouthed at him. For a woman a thousand years old (rounding down), not a good look.

She shut her mouth with a snap and directed her gaze to the ground.

Where she couldn't help but notice his narrow-toed shoes were highly shined.

And felt fat and frumpy by contrast. And of course, at that moment, noticed some kind of stain on the skirt of her suit.

Typical.

He must be a god.

But not one she'd met before; he couldn't possibly be human looking that good.

She recovered herself enough to mumble, "thank you," and shuffled a little further away from the scent of hot clean body that she really shouldn't have been able to appreciate in that wind.

And yet, it was as if he carried a tiny cloud of stillness with him, that left him completely unaffected by the troubles of ordinary men.

Another reason to label him a god and back away while she could.

"You should be careful," he said, "texting while you walk is never a good idea."

The traffic lights sounded don't walk.

"Of course. I'm sorry to trouble you," she risked looking up at him as a large truck barrelled around the corner.

And heard the sickening sound of a phone being ground beneath three double sets of tyres.

Her face paled and she clenched and unclenched her left hand - the emptiness told her it was *her* phone in pieces on its way down the street.

And her life with it.

Not that it was that hard to get a new phone, but it might be years before she managed to get a new one set up with universal roaming and all her favourite apps.

Especially the ones she couldn't remember the passwords for.

And the ones she used to keep herself occupied when her sisters were quarrelling.

She closed her eyes and started enunciating as many swearwords as she could think of.

Quietly, in her mind, less the god thought she was common.

"I'm so sorry," he said, "I didn't mean for you to use your phone. Let me buy you a new one."

She sighed; partly from sorrow, and partly because she feared for her sanity should she spend any more time with him than she had to.

"No thanks, it's my fault. I'm just thankful it was my phone and not me under that truck."

"I insist."

"No really, it's fine."

The traffic lights signalled walk again, "I must go," she said, "I can't be late back to work as well."

And with that lie, she ran down the street as fast as her pencil skirt and stilettos would let her.

Slowing down as she ducked through an arcade, down some stairs, and into the dark, beery scented recesses of her favourite wine bar.

After that embarrassment, she *needed* several very large, very strong alcoholic drinks.

The bar was the place she spent most of her time, and she tended to think of it as her office.

After all, she was there most of the day, and well into the evening.

It seemed easier and less stressful to get things done than at home.

Which was almost fair enough because as well as more cluttered than she could stand, her home also contained her sisters.

Whereas the bar was blissfully free of both sisters and clutter.

If she hadn't needed her sisters as much as they needed her, she would have moved out.

Come to think of it, these days they spent a lot of time apart.

Wouldn't it be more practical for them to share an apartment building than a house?

Then they could all get a bit of space when they needed to get away from each other.

It was just not possible she was the only sister who got annoyed by their constant close proximity.

Then again, so far as she knew, none of them knew how far they could get from each other.

Or for how long.

She smiled at the barman as she walked in, and he asked, "the usual?"

Laura nodded on her way through to her favourite table; the one in a small alcove where she could sit with her back to the wall, and her face towards the door.

The lights were a little dim, which gave her a sense of privacy.

The wooden floors could have made the space echo, but the plush chairs and curtains around the walls absorbed much of the noise.

Most of the patrons were middle-ageish, and most just wanted somewhere for a quiet drink, so the sound of conversation was muted.

While she waited for her Negroni and charcuterie plate, she slipped her shoes off, ignoring how difficult they would be to get them back on.

Then wriggled her toes and flexed her ankles.

At the same time, she took a deep breath and held it while she rocked her head back and forth across her shoulders, then rotated each shoulder back opening up the sockets.

When she felt slightly less stressed, she started looking for her backup device.

Also known as The Notebook, complete with a slim black and silver fountain pen attached to the cover with an elastic band.

Without the phone, those who wanted her would be drawn to the bar, and she'd need the book to record their wishes in.

It was never a conscious choice to open for business, (so to speak), but that people just started arriving when she was ready for them.

And whatever the reason, they just told her their life stories.

Laura laid her notebook on the table before her, opened up to a new blank page, and tucked the fountain pen between the pages to mark her place.

From her position, there were several tables between her and the door, which allowed her the opportunity to observe punters as they came in.

They were generally recognisable by the way they meandered through the bar, always stopping for a quick shot of liquid courage on their way.

She took a sip of her drink and speared a piece of bresaola, as she watched a man approach.

She didn't actually listen to what he said, but observed what she saw.

In the old days she'd look through clients to the weave of their threads. The weft showed where they'd been and were headed, and the warp the obstacles in their path. And when she'd seen the lay of the weave, she'd twitch it.

But it took them years to come and go, and by the time they'd got to her, the cloth would have sorted itself out.

As time went by, they moved a little faster, taking only months to find her.

They'd stopped thinking of themselves as tapestries and started thinking of themselves as books.

She learned to read them, editing the details to change their endings.

Modern life, by comparison, was exhaustingly instant, and modern people thought of themselves as movies. She'd taught herself to scroll through their lives, editing, erasing, or sometimes allowing a second take.

But more people wanted more dramatic edits, and they wanted them more often.

To distract the time-wasters she'd seeded ideas through the universes. The quick fixes offered by magazines and influencers took some of the load, leaving her free to focus on the complex issues.

Which it had to be said, were generally more interesting.

The man, seemingly satisfied, left. She noted the details so she'd remember them to pass them onto her sister Agatha.

Not that it mattered, Agatha could see the future while Laura only saw the present.

A woman was next, then another man, and another.

And after a while, she lost track of how many there were.

Laura sighed, closed her eyes, and rotated her head on her shoulders again.

It was time to call it a day.

She was tired, grumpy about the phone, and wanted to relax in a hot bath.

Just one more client...

Then she'd call it a day.

She could read this guy with her eyes closed; drinks, dinner, leading to marriage, kids, hand-holding in old age.

Laura found the woman he was thinking about weirdly familiar.

And there was something about his cologne.

She opened her eyes and found herself looking into the green eyes of the guy who'd put her back on her feet that morning.

He said nothing, just looked at her.

Judging her?

Or her reaction to him.

Hard to say with that inscrutable face.

She thought about what he'd probably seen.

A bunch of people coming to her table one by one, stopping for a short time, then leaving while she made notes in The Notebook.

And as she laid down her pen, the next person arrived.

Was he thinking bookmaking?

Drugs?

Prostitution?

For a moment she fretted about what he thought she'd been up to.

And then she realised it was none of his bloody business.

She frowned.

"That's my girl," he said and leant forward to lay a hand on hers.

Instantly, they were standing halfway up a mountain somewhere.

Definitely a god then.

A god with nothing better to do with his time than spend it bugging her.

A god who looked insanely attractive in jeans and a tight green sweater that matched his eyes.

She sucked in a breath of crisp clear air and looked around her.

The sun shone in a clear sky; a little off centre, so sometime late morning or early afternoon.

The dark grey rocky slope beneath her suggested volcano (hopefully extinct), and she looked up to see snow on the peaks; seemingly close enough to walk to.

A gentle breeze caressed her hair, and when she reached up to smooth it back, she realised she was wearing blue jeans and a red plaid flannel button-down shirt.

She shuddered with discomfort at the garish outfit.

Now that she'd seen it, she couldn't not see it, and soon it seemed that all she could see was a red plaid flannel pillow encompassing the world.

She couldn't think with all that noise going on.

A gust of wind set her hair flying, and when she tried to get it back under control, she realised it was longer than before.

The bloody cheek of him.

She patted her pockets and found nothing in them.

A quick glance at her feet revealed chestnut coloured hiking boots, but no bag, and no Notebook.

Had he perhaps *deliberately* thrown her phone under the truck?

For a moment she panicked, then remembered that her sister Claudia saw the past, and with Agatha seeing the future, they should be able to track her down soon enough.

"Why would you want your sisters to track you?" he asked. "Haven't you wanted to get away from them for centuries?"

She folded arms and glared at him.

He shrugged, "I think you should leap at the chance to lead that ordinary life you've been thinking about."

"I don't see much ordinary about shacking up with a god who's got tickets on himself," she snapped.

If it wasn't bad enough that he'd changed her clothes and messed with her hair, now he was telling her what to do?

He laughed, "I could do with a hot chocolate, how about you?" He grabbed her hand and started walking down the mountain towards what looked like a ski lift station.

She tried to pull her hand free with little success.

And wondered very quietly, could he really read her mind?

Or was he predicting her reaction based on what he knew about her?

And how long exactly had he known about her while she had no notion about him?

Stalker much?

He knew she had sisters, but did he know who they were?

Or regardless of how much they detested each other in any given moment, how much they needed each other?

Still trying to detach her hand, but this time to help maintain her balance, she followed him into the station café.

Obviously, they were the only ones in the place. Not even anyone behind the counter.

Was it possible he could stop time?

He went behind the espresso machine to froth milk and pour it over some shaved chocolate in large ceramic mugs.

Thought he was so bloody smart.

It would take more than a man who knew his way around a coffee machine to impress her.

She wandered into the kitchen, trying not to arouse his suspicion, and finding a large kitchen knife she used it to hack her hair into a ragged bob.

Leaving the excess on the floor, she wandered back to the main café.

Only this time she walked into a wall of noise produced by one hundred hyperactive children. "Mummy, mummy," they shouted and latched onto her legs, and she counted them at five.

Five children somewhere between the ages of five and ten.

Or given the way god children aged, anywhere between five and five hundred.

Five children who laughed as they reached back to grab her the minute she prised them off her.

She turned to see where the god was, and he was sitting in an overstuffed armchair in a lounge room.

"What the ffff...," even though these were not really children, she tried to think of a clean word to use.

"What the fudge?"

"Isn't this what you wanted? A home of your own, a husband and children?"

"Not all on the same day!"

She rocked on her feet as the children disappeared.

"And not like this," she continued, flinging her right arm up to encompass him and his armchair, "but the old-fashioned way. The way humans do it. Meeting. Dating. Gifts. Falling in love."

"Are you sure? Sounds tedious."

She sank into herself, "I'm sure."

The room disappeared, and she was sitting at her table in the bar again. Trying to work out what had just happened.

But the more desperately she tried to remember it, the more quickly it slipped away.

《《 • 》》

She sighed, closed her eyes, and rotated her head on her shoulders.

It was time to call it a day.

She was tired, grumpy about the phone, and wanted to relax in a hot bath.

Just one more client...

Then she'd call it a day.

She could read this guy with her eyes closed; drinks, dinner, leading to marriage, kids, hand-holding in old age.

His cologne was fresh and citrusy. There was something familiar about it.

She opened her eyes and found herself look-ing into the green eyes of the guy who'd put her back on her feet that morning.

"Oh," she said.

"I wasn't sure it was you, but I thought I'd stop by and see."

"It's me all right," she closed The Notebook, slipping the pen into its elastic and put it in her bag.

He put a small box on the table, "I felt really bad about your phone so I got you another one."

Laura rested her hands on the table but didn't touch the box.

"How did you know I would be here?"

"I didn't. I just dropped in here for a drink be-fore heading home. It must be Fate."

She managed not to roll her eyes at the corny chat up line.

He nudged the box closer to her, "please take it."

She sighed and reached out for the box, "thank you?"

"Eurus, my name's Eurus."

Definitely a god then, and still using his true name.

"Laura." He might know hers, but she and her sisters had agreed to go incognito.

"Can I get you another drink Laura?" He glanced at his watch, "or seeing as it's getting late, maybe some dinner?"

She should go home, but the evening had just got interesting. She threw the box in her bag, "why not? Let's get out of here."

THE END

As a small token of my thanks for reading...

Please enjoy 10% off everything (excluding shipping)

at alexandriablaelock.com

with the code lauraten.

Turn the page for some ideas where to use it,

Life interrupted

To say the letter was a surprise was an understatement. It arrived addressed to Miss Finlay Cox, which made the contents even more extraordinary.

Orphan Finn Cox inherits a cottage. Thinks it holds the key to her origins. Of course she takes a look. Who wouldn't?

But when she gets there, she gets more than she bargained for.

Is it friend, family or foe?

All she wants is a place of her own.

When Alison Porter finds a tiny cottage for sale, she thinks her dreams have come true. Inside virgin bushland, "Crow Cottage" sits on the smallest parcel of cleared land.

It's old. It's run down. It's keeping a secret.

Stumbling through a mysterious portal in the garden, she finds herself in a place of mystery and intrigue. As the past, present and future collide, she must unravel the secret, for only then can she reweave the tapestry of time.

If you love a story of twists and turns, where nothing is what it seems, grab Weaving the Wildwood today

Meet Morag Clementine. The new housekeeper at historic Hayward Hall.

Her practical and capable attitude usually keeps her out of trouble.

bove all, her no-nonsense, get it done approach. And her get in the middle of the scrum outlook. Just as well, because Hayward Hall needs someone like her.

In this genre-spanning collection of original stories, Morag finds herself ensnared in the History of Hayward Hall...

No ordinary housekeeper, can Morag save the house, one century at a time?

Perhaps you'll carry your new books
in one of these bags

Enjoy them while drinking from
one of these mugs

Or wearing one of these t-shirts

ABOUT THE AUTHOR

Australian author Alexandria Blaelock writes mostly fantasy and mystery.

She's appeared in the Stringybark Anthology *Crowd Surfing*, *Pulphouse Fiction Magazine*, and *Ellery Queen's Mystery Magazine*.

She's also written five self-help books applying business techniques to personal matters like getting dressed, tidying up, and feeding friends.

When not exploring parallel universes, she talks to animals, indulges in K-dramas, and sips Campari. She lives in the Dandenongs, where she relishes the sound of birdsong, the scent of gum leaves and the sun on her face.

Discover more at https://alexandriablaelock.com.